Dear Parents:

Congratulations! Your child is taking the first steps on an exciting journey. The destination? Independent reading!

STEP INTO READING® will help your child get there. The program offers five steps to reading success. Each step includes fun stories and colorful art or photographs. In addition to original fiction and books with favorite characters, there are Step into Reading Non-Fiction Readers, Phonics Readers and Boxed Sets, Sticker Readers, and Comic Readers—a complete literacy program with something to interest every child.

Learning to Read, Step by Step!

Ready to Read   Preschool–Kindergarten
• big type and easy words • rhyme and rhythm • picture clues
For children who know the alphabet and are eager to begin reading.

Reading with Help   Preschool–Grade 1
• basic vocabulary • short sentences • simple stories
For children who recognize familiar words and sound out new words with help.

Reading on Your Own   Grades 1–3
• engaging characters • easy-to-follow plots • popular topics
For children who are ready to read on their own.

Reading Paragraphs   Grades 2–3
• challenging vocabulary • short paragraphs • exciting stories
For newly independent readers who read simple sentences with confidence.

Ready for Chapters   Grades 2–4
• chapters • longer paragraphs • full-color art
For children who want to take the plunge into chapter books but still like colorful pictures.

STEP INTO READING® is designed to give every child a successful reading experience. The grade levels are only guides; children will progress through the steps at their own speed, developing confidence in their reading.

Remember, a lifetime love of reading starts with a single step!

To my husband, Tim, with love
—M.B.

For my nephew, Walter
—K.E.

Text copyright © 2024 by Margaret Buckley
Cover art and interior illustrations copyright © 2024 by Kiersten Eagan

All rights reserved. Published in the United States by Random House Children's Books, a division of Penguin Random House LLC, New York.

Step into Reading, Random House, and the Random House colophon are registered trademarks of Penguin Random House LLC.

Visit us on the Web!
StepIntoReading.com
rhcbooks.com

Educators and librarians, for a variety of teaching tools, visit us at RHTeachersLibrarians.com

Library of Congress Cataloging-in-Publication Data is available upon request.
ISBN 978-0-593-80776-7 (trade) — ISBN 978-0-593-80777-4 (lib. bdg.) —
ISBN 978-0-593-80778-1 (ebook)

Printed in the United States of America
10 9 8 7 6 5 4 3 2 1
First Edition

Ice Cream Town

by Margaret Buckley
illustrated by Kiersten Eagan

Random House 🏠 New York

I want to live in
Ice Cream Town.

Everywhere you look
around—
ice cream up and
ice cream down.
I want to live in
Ice Cream Town.

Ice Cream Town has
an ice cream train.

It chugs along
on Ice Cream Lane.

It chugs in the sun

and the snow

and the rain.

Ice Cream Town has
an ice cream train.

Ice Cream Town has
ice cream streets.

All the houses
are made of sweets!

Each house has
some special treats.
Ice Cream Town has
ice cream streets.

Ice Cream Town has
an ice cream shop.
I like ice cream and
I cannot stop!

Hot fudge sundae
with a cherry on top.
Ice Cream Town has
an ice cream shop.

Ice Cream Town has
ice cream stores.
I like ice cream and
I want some more!

Ice cream roofs and
ice cream floors.
Ice Cream Town has
ice cream stores.

Ice Cream Town has
an ice cream school
with an ice cream gym
and an ice cream pool.

An ice cream school
is really cool!
Ice Cream Town has
an ice cream school.

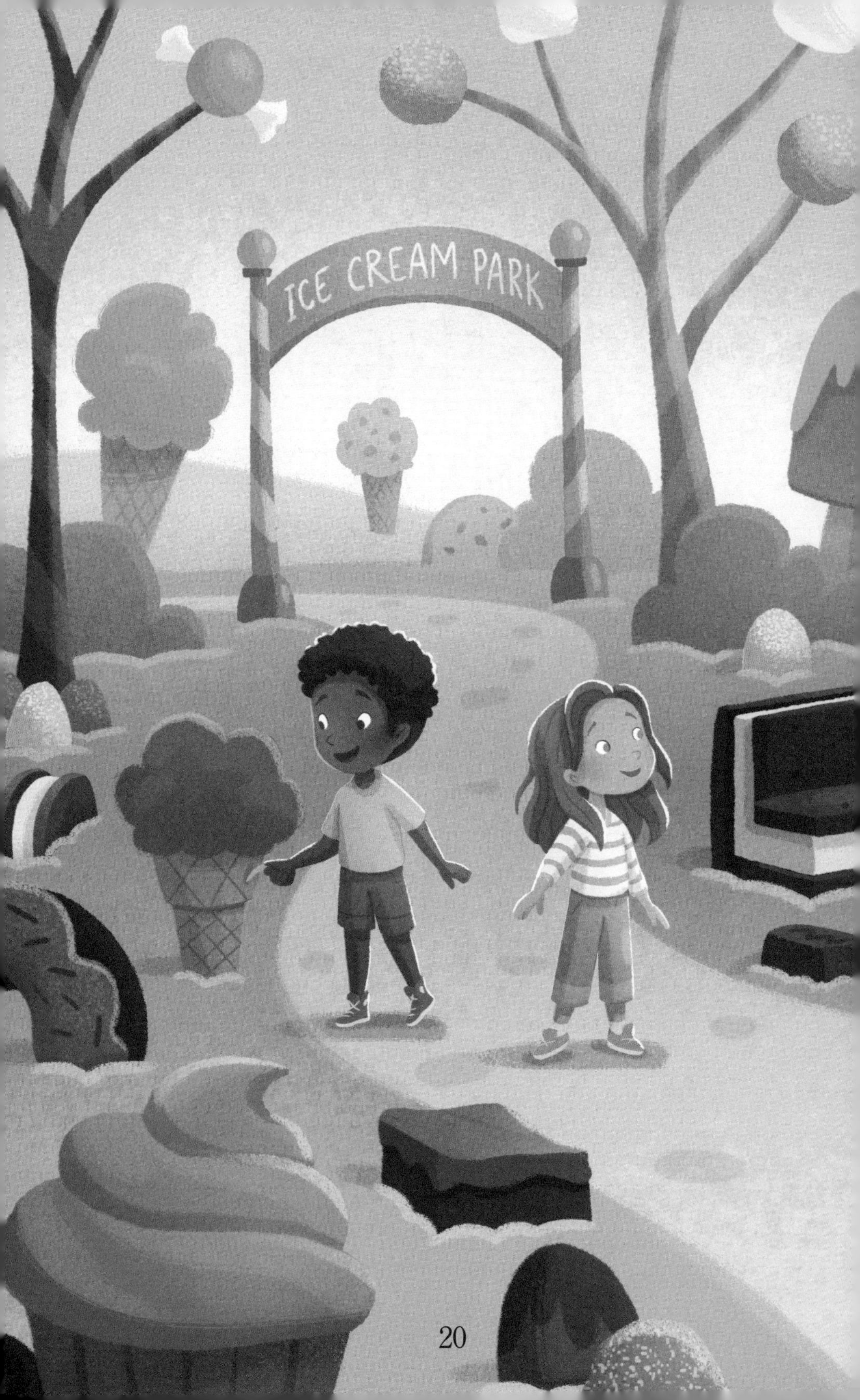
ICE CREAM PARK

Ice Cream Town has
an ice cream park.
The ice cream trees
have ice cream bark!

Play in the daylight.

Play in the dark.

Ice Cream Town has
an ice cream park.

Ice Cream Park has an ice cream slide.

On ice cream,
it is fun to glide!
Take a
slippery ice cream ride!
Ice Cream Park has
an ice cream slide.

Ice Cream Park has
an ice cream swing.
Swings add fun
to everything!

Summer, winter,
fall, and spring.
Ice Cream Park has
an ice cream swing.

Ice Cream Town has
an ice cream lake.
Sea of ice cream
and a shore of cake.

Sit and take

an ice cream break!

Ice Cream Town has

an ice cream lake.

Let's all live in
Ice Cream Town!
Everywhere you look
around—
ice cream up and
ice cream down.

Let's all live in
Ice Cream Town!